Rescues in Focus

# Underground Rescues

by Mark L. Lewis

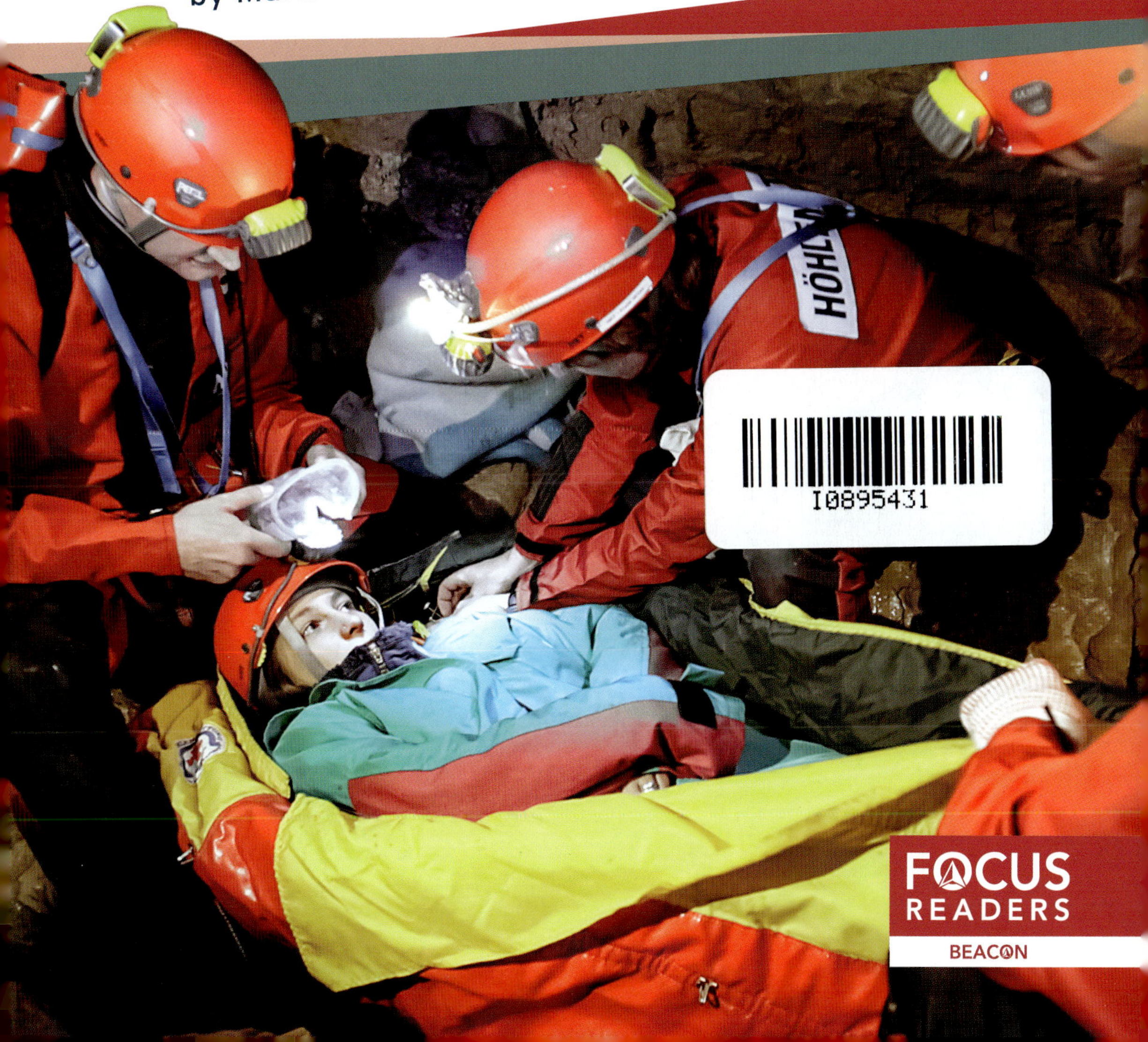



FOCUS READERS

BEACON

www.focusreaders.com



Focus Readers is distributed by North Star Editions:
sales@northstareditions.com | 888-417-0195

Produced for Focus Readers by Red Line Editorial.

Photographs ©: Marijan_Murat/picture-alliance/dpa/AP Images, cover, 1; Sakchai Lalit/AP Images, 4; Linh Pham/Getty Images News/Getty Images, 7, 29; Thai Navy/Polaris/Newscom, 9; Cpl. Adam Dublinske/US Marine Corps/Defense Visual Information Distribution Service, 10; Mass Communication Specialist 1st Class Abe McNatt/US Navy, 13; Senior Airman Ryan Conroy/US Air Force/Defense Visual Information Distribution Service, 14; aetb/iStockphoto, 17; Jorge Saenz/AP Images, 18–19, 23; Rott70/iStockphoto, 20; pedrosala/Shutterstock Images, 25 (left); Berenika_L/iStockphoto, 25 (right); Bai Yu/Xinhua/AP Images, 27

**Library of Congress Cataloging-in-Publication Data**
Names: Lewis, Mark L., 1991- author.
Title: Underground rescues / by Mark L. Lewis.
Description: Lake Elmo, MN : Focus Readers, [2020] | Series: Rescues in focus | Audience: Grades 4-6. | Includes bibliographical references and index. |
Identifiers: LCCN 2019011218 (print) | LCCN 2019011982 (ebook) | ISBN 9781641859820 (pdf) | ISBN 9781641859134 (ebook) | ISBN 9781641857758 (hardcover) | ISBN 9781641858441 (pbk.)
Subjects: LCSH: Special forces (Military science)--United States--Juvenile literature. | Caving--Search and rescue operations--Juvenile literature. | Mine rescue work--Juvenile literature.
Classification: LCC UA34.S64 (ebook) | LCC UA34.S64 L486 2020 (print) | DDC 363.34/81--dc23
LC record available at https://lccn.loc.gov/2019011218

Printed in the United States of America
Mankato, MN
May, 2019

# About the Author

Mark L. Lewis lives in Minnesota but has traveled all over the world. He loves writing books for young readers.

# Table of Contents

Chapter 1

# Trapped in a Cave

In 2018, a soccer team in Thailand set out to explore a cave. The boys left their bikes at the cave's entrance. They had explored the cave many times before. They did not plan on being gone for long.

**The Tham Luang cave system is one of the biggest in Thailand.**

But soon, rainwater started filling the cave. The boys were trapped. They were 2.5 miles (4.0 km) from the entrance.

A rescue **mission** quickly formed. But saving the boys would be difficult. The cave's passages were narrow. Also, the water flooding the

### Did You Know?

**Thailand's rainy season can last from May to October. Floodwaters can rise to 16 feet (4.9 m) high in caves.**

Divers sometimes come from around the world to help with rescue efforts.

cave was muddy. Divers could not see through it.

After a week of searching, divers found the team. The boys were still alive. But rescuers did not know how to get them out of the cave.

Most of the boys could not swim. And they did not know how to use diving gear.

A few days later, the rescuers had a plan. First, they put each boy to sleep using a drug. Next, they put an air mask on each boy. Each mask was connected to an

## Did You Know?

**People can last without food for several weeks. But they can last for only a few days without fresh water.**

**Thai soldiers bring a supply of air tanks to boys trapped in a cave.**

air tank. Then, divers carried the boys through the flooded cave.

The divers had to go slow. It took them three days to rescue everyone. But the boys were finally safe. They had been trapped for two weeks.

Chapter 2

# Becoming a Rescuer

Underground rescuers are often members of the military. Most countries have military groups that **specialize** in difficult rescues. These groups train to stay calm in tough situations.

**A US soldier practices moving through a tight space with an air tank.**

The United States has the Navy **SEALs**. It also has **pararescue** teams. Both groups go through hard training. The soldiers have to be in excellent health. They have to pass many physical tests. These tests push the limits of what the soldiers can do.

Navy SEAL training can take more than two years. SEALs learn scuba diving and medical skills. They train to be leaders. As they train, they build up their **stamina**.

Navy SEALs learn how to work through the worst conditions.

Underground rescues can be stressful. For example, underground passages can be tight and dark. There is no room for error. Soldiers learn to stay focused.

**US soldiers practice sharing one air tank. This rescue skill is called buddy breathing.**

Pararescue training takes nearly two years. The soldiers are called PJs. They spend the day doing land exercises and drills. Then they go to a training area called the Pool.

At the Pool, PJs learn how to take off and put on scuba gear. They learn how to tie knots. They learn hand-to-hand fighting. But they practice all these skills underwater. And they practice them all without breathing. This training helps PJs stay calm underwater.

## Did You Know?

**Only 20 percent of soldiers make it through PJ training. Some soldiers quit. Others fail the tests.**

Not all underground rescuers are part of the military. Some rescuers are highly trained scuba divers. Rescue divers spend many hours training in the water. They know how to keep people calm during a rescue. They also know how to carry **unconscious** people

## Did You Know?

**In 2014, 728 people spent 12 days rescuing a man in Germany. It was one of the largest underground rescue missions ever.**

Rescue divers try to keep unconscious victims' necks straight on the way to the surface.

to safety. These skills are especially important for rescue divers in flooded caves.

THAT'S AMAZING!

# Underground for 69 Days

Disaster struck Chile in 2010. A mine collapsed, trapping 33 men. The men were able to move to a safe area. They had some food. But the food was meant to last only two days. The men would be trapped for 69 days.

Rescuers knew where the trapped men were. The hard part was getting them out. Eventually, rescuers drilled a hole. They lowered a tube approximately 2,000 feet (600 m) into the mine. The tube was only 28 inches (71 cm) wide. The men squeezed into the tube one at a time. All the men made it out of the mine safely.

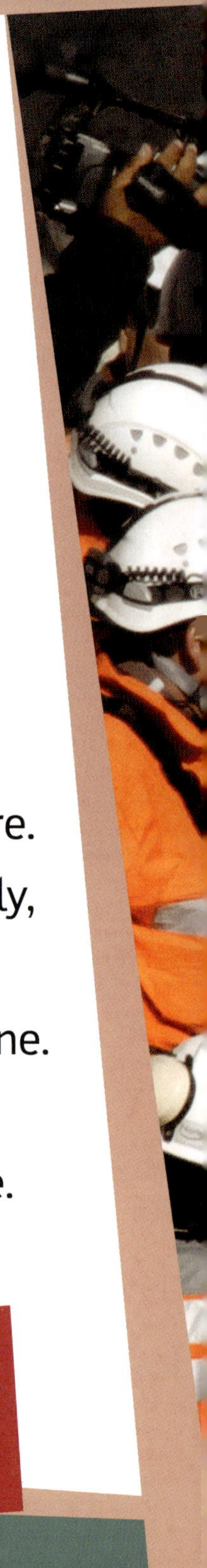

A Chilean miner exits a tube after being trapped.

FENIX 2

Chapter 3

# On the Job

Underground rescues can take a long time. Rescuers do not always know where people are trapped. Rescuers might need to spend time searching around the area. But they act as fast as they can.

**Because they are underground, rescue divers often have to swim in near darkness.**

People who are trapped often have little food or water. They may also have limited access to air.

Sometimes rescuers have to get creative. They may need to use drills to reach the victims. But mines and caves can collapse. So drillers have to be careful.

**Did You Know?**

**In 1987, a toddler fell into a well. Rescuers lowered a microphone into the well to see if she was alive. They heard the toddler's voice. Rescuers saved her.**

**In 2010, rescuers drilled for more than a month to reach trapped miners in Chile.**

Scientists can also help on rescue missions. For instance, **engineers** know how to use specialized tools. **Geologists** understand how mountains and cave systems work.

Together, these scientists can find the safest way for rescuers to reach people.

Once a safe route is found, rescuers put on their gear. Rescue divers wear wet suits, flippers, and goggles. They also put on air tanks. This gear lets them move through flooded caves.

Other rescuers might wear helmets, headlamps, and thick gloves. The helmets protect them from falling rock. The headlamps

help them see where they are going. The gloves protect their hands.

Rescuers also bring ropes with them. The ropes can act as guides. Caves often have many tunnels. It can be easy for people to get lost. Rescuers lay down ropes as they go.

That way, they can follow the ropes back to the cave's entrance.

Rescuers may bring **harnesses** with the ropes, too. Cave walls may be too steep to climb out of. In that case, rescuers put people in harnesses. Using ropes, they lift those people to the cave's surface.

Trapped victims might also be injured. Rescuers often use **stretchers** to safely carry victims out. Doctors may enter the cave or mine, too. Doctors find the injured

A miner is rescued on a stretcher after a coal mine flooded in China.

victims. They work to stabilize them until they can be rescued.

Underground, many things can go wrong. Rescuers can get hurt during rescues, too. But rescuers use their skills and tools to help as many people as they can.

FOCUS ON

# Underground Rescues

*Write your answers on a separate piece of paper.*

1. Write a sentence describing the main idea of Chapter 2.
2. Engineers, geologists, divers, and more work together on rescue missions. Which role would you prefer? Why?
3. What type of scientist sometimes helps in underground rescues?
   - **A.** a Navy SEAL
   - **B.** a geologist
   - **C.** a pararescuer
4. Which rescue location would require scuba divers as part of the rescue team?
   - **A.** a steep cave
   - **B.** a collapsed mine
   - **C.** a flooded cave

**5.** What does **physical** mean in this book?

*The soldiers have to be in excellent health. They have to pass many **physical** tests.*

- **A.** having to do with the body
- **B.** having to do with the mind
- **C.** having to do with school

**6.** What does **stabilize** mean in this book?

*Doctors find the injured victims. They work to **stabilize** them until they can be rescued.*

- **A.** to fully treat all of the patients' injuries
- **B.** to ask patients questions about their injuries
- **C.** to keep patients' injuries from getting worse

*Answer key on page 32.*

# Glossary

**engineers**
People who design and create buildings or machines.

**geologists**
Scientists who study Earth's crust.

**harnesses**
Pieces of equipment that hold things in place.

**mission**
An important task or operation.

**pararescue**
A search-and-rescue mission carried out by trained professionals.

**SEALs**
Highly trained soldiers who carry out special operations.

**specialize**
To be involved in a particular type of activity.

**stamina**
The ability to continue working for a long time.

**stretchers**
Medical devices used to carry sick or injured people.

**unconscious**
Not awake; passed out.

# To Learn More

## BOOKS

Hamilton, S. L. *Search & Rescue.* Minneapolis: Abdo Publishing, 2016.

Olson, Sonja. *Caves.* Lake Elmo, MN: Focus Readers, 2018.

Pearson, Yvonne. *The Chilean Miners: Buried Alive.* Mankato, MN: The Child's World, 2016.

## NOTE TO EDUCATORS

Visit **www.focusreaders.com** to find lesson plans, activities, links, and other resources related to this title.

# Index



**Answer Key: 1.** Answers will vary; **2.** Answers will vary; **3.** B; **4.** C; **5.** A; **6.** C